A Christmas Alphabet Book

by Lisa Bullard

illustrated by Joni Oeltjenbruns

 Carolrhoda Books, Inc./Minneapolis

Special thanks to Vicki Revsbech:
Not Enough Ways! to say thank you—LB

Text copyright © 1999 by Lisa Bullard
Illustrations copyright © 1999 by Joni Oeltjenbruns

Carolrhoda Books, Inc.
A Division of the Lerner Publishing Group
241 First Avenue North
Minneapolis, MN 55401 U.S.A.

Website address: www.lernerbooks.com

Library of Congress Cataloging-in-Publication Data

Bullard, Lisa.
   Not Enough Beds! : A Christmas alphabet book / by Lisa Bullard ;
illustrated by Joni Oeltjenbruns.
      p.   cm.
   Summary: Zachary goes through the alphabet recounting who sleeps
where, from Aunt Alison in an overstuffed chair to himself under the
tree, when all the relatives come to visit at Christmas.
   ISBN 1-57505-356-X (alk. paper)
   [1. Beds—Fiction. 2. Bedtime—Fiction. 3. Christmas—Fiction. 4.
Alphabet. 5. Stories in rhyme.] I. Oeltjenbruns, Joni, ill. II. Title.
PZ8.3.B885No 1999
[E]—dc21   98-30518

Manufactured in the United States of America
1 2 3 4 5 6 – JR – 04 03 02 01 00 99

*For my family, who were my first and best friends,
and for my friends, who are now a part of my family:
there are always extra beds for you at my house.*

—L.B.

*Dedicated to Doug, Mikaela, Devan, Kade, Dayna,
and Matalin—my family, my joy!*

—J.O.

*C*hristmas is coming—no, Christmas is here!

And there's just one small problem

with this time of year.

When all of the family comes here to stay,

we can't go to sleep in the usual way…

So Aunt **A**lison snores in an overstuffed chair,

while my young brother **B**en
stretches out on a stair.

Smart Cousin **Constantine**
brought his own cot,

and the porch swing's just perfect

for little Aunt **D**ot.

Mistletoe beckons
to shy Uncle **Ed**,

while big Uncle **Fritz**
makes a snow-angel bed.

Grandpa tells yarns

that make **Hank**, my dad, yawn.

Isaac and **J**esse play Go Fish till dawn.

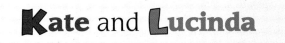

Kate and **L**ucinda
hide under a table,

while sugarplums romp

through the dreams of Aunt **Mabel**.

My vain sister **Nan**

curls her hair up too tight.

Bold Uncle **Orland**

sings "O Holy Night."

There's a star-bright night-light
in the upstairs front hall
specifically shining
for new baby **Paul**.

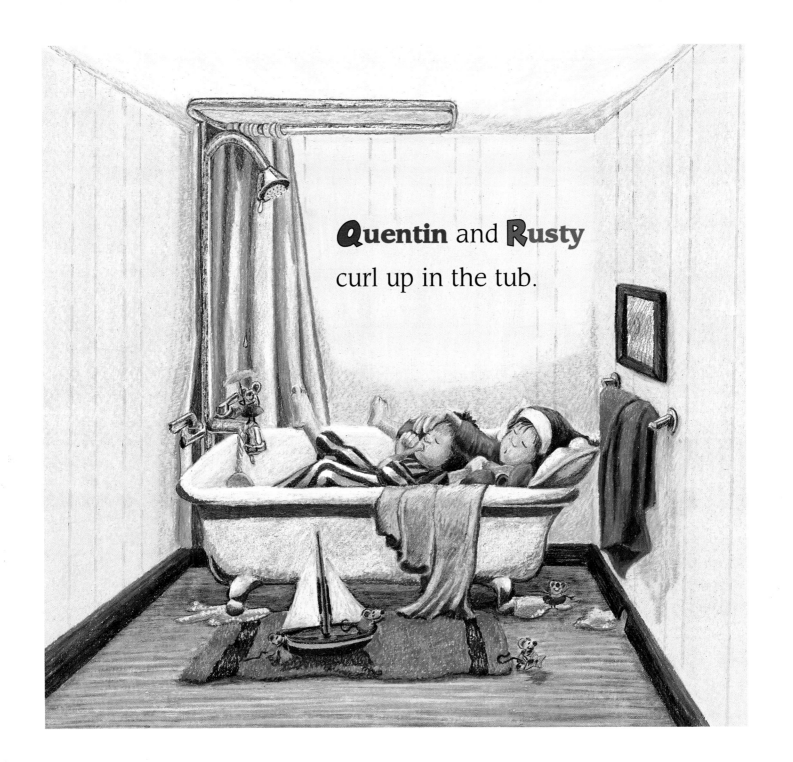

Quentin and **R**usty

curl up in the tub.

My mom, **Sally**, and **Tim** cause a kitchen hubbub.

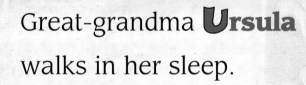

Great-grandma **Ursula**
walks in her sleep.

Victoria stands on her head and counts sheep.

Winnifred, **Xylo**, and **Yancy** the dogs
pile up by the fire like a heap of old logs.

And me?

In this Christmas Eve crowd

I'm much harder to see,

but here I am . . .

. . . **Z**achary, under the tree!